D1492309

Another one for my Hazel(nut),
who I hope always finds a home in my books
—GL

For my parents, who indulged all of my bookish escapes
—KM

ABOUT THIS BOOK

The illustrations for this book were done in gouache on Arches hot press Watercolor Paper. This book was edited by Alvina Ling and designed by Patrick Collins with art direction from Saho Fujii. The production was supervised by Kimberly Stella, and the production editor was Annie McDonnell. The text was set in Adobe Caslon Pro, and the display type is hand lettering.

Text copyright © 2023 by Grace Lin and Kate Messner • Illustrations copyright © 2023 by Grace Lin • Cover illustration copyright © 2023 by Grace Lin • Cover design by Patrick Collins • Cover copyright © 2023 by Hachette Book Group, Inc. • Hachette Book Group supports the right to free expression and the value of copyright. The purpose of copyright is to encourage writers and artists to produce the creative works that enrich our culture. • The scanning, uploading, and distribution of this book without permission is a theft of the author's intellectual property. If you would like permission to use material from the book (other than for review purposes), please contact permissions@hbgusa.com. Thank you for your support of the author's rights. • Little, Brown and Company • Hachette Book Group • 1290 Avenue of the Americas, New York, NY 10104 • Visit us at LBYR.com • First Edition: February 2023 • Little, Brown and Company is a division of Hachette Book Group, Inc. • The Little, Brown name and logo are trademarks of Hachette Book Group, Inc. • The publisher is not responsible for websites (or their content) that are not owned by the publisher. • Library of Congress Cataloging-in-Publication Data • Names: Lin, Grace, author, illustrator. | Messner, Kate, author. • Title: Once upon a book / written by Grace Lin and Kate Messner ; art by Grace Lin. • Description: First edition. | New York : Little, Brown and Company, 2022. | Audience: Ages 4–8. | Summary: A little girl named Alice opens a book on a rainy day and travels around the world through its pages. • Identifiers: LCCN 2021016142 | ISBN 9780316541077 (hardcover) • Subjects: CYAC: Books and reading—Fiction. | Home—Fiction. • Classification: LCC PZ7.L644 On 2022 | DDC [E]—dc23 • LC record available at https://lccn.loc.gov/2021016142 • ISBN 978-0-316-54107-7 • PRINTED IN CHINA • APS • 10 9 8 7 6 5 4 3 2 1

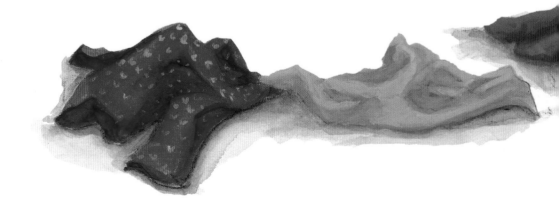

Once Upon a Book

By **Grace Lin**
and **Kate Messner**

Illustrated by
Grace Lin

L B

LITTLE, BROWN AND COMPANY
New York   Boston

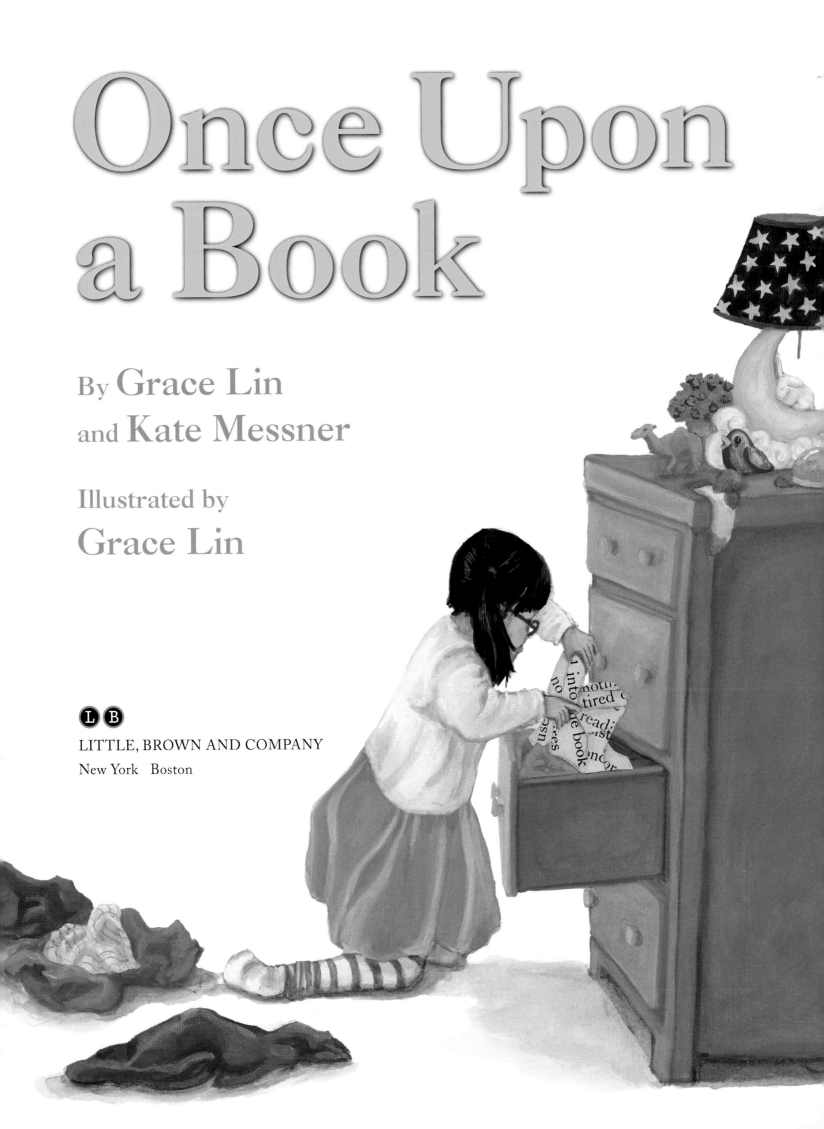

Alice was tired of heavy sweaters and thick socks and staying inside with nothing to do. "I wish I were someplace that wasn't so frozen and gray!" she grumbled to her mother.

She began to stomp away, but something flapped nearby. It was the pages of a book. Curious, Alice began to read.

Once upon a time, there was a girl, Alice read. She went to a place alive with colors, where even the morning dew was warm.

"That sounds like our home," said the birds. "Turn the page and come in...."

So she did.

The air felt as if it came from an oven, the book said. *The girl and the birds played among the flowers.*

But then the rains
came down.

"I wish I were someplace that wasn't
so steamy and drippy," Alice said.

With the book over
her head, Alice read,

*So the girl went to a place
of sparkling sands, where
the sun would dry her.*

"That sounds like our home," said the camels. "Turn the page and come in...."

So she did.

The sun blazed down and dried
her hair as she rode on a camel
through the desert.

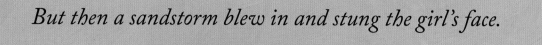

But then a sandstorm blew in and stung the girl's face.

"I wish I were someplace that wasn't so dusty and dry."
Then, Alice read, *So the girl went to a place of clear waters,*
where the sea would refresh her.

"That sounds like our home," said the fish.
"Turn the page and come in...."

So she did.

The gentle water soothed her as she swam
with the fish through the coral reefs.

But the girl got tangled in seaweed.
She was caught and confused.

"I wish I were someplace that wasn't so
cramped and crowded." Then, Alice read,
So the girl went to a place of wide-open blue,
where she would be boundless and free.

"That sounds like our home,"
said the clouds. "Turn the page
and come in...."

So she did.

The clouds billowed like the sails of a ship.
The girl rode the wind through the sky.

But the clouds darkened and the thunder roared.

"I wish I were someplace that wasn't so booming and loud!"

So the girl went to a place with no sounds at all, Alice read, *where she could be quiet and calm.*

"That sounds like my house,"
whispered the moon.
"Turn the page and
come visit."

"That sounds like my home," whispered the moon.
"Turn the page and come in…."

So she did.

The soundless stars twinkled and winked as she floated
in the moon's glowing light.

But the emptiness made the girl feel alone.

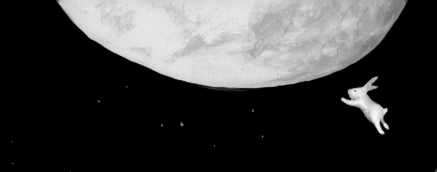

"I wish I were someplace that wasn't so lonely," Alice thought.

So the girl went to a place of coziness and warmth, where the kitchen smelled of dumplings and her family was waiting with dinner.

"That sounds like my home," Alice said.

"Turn the page," her mother said,
"and come in...."

And so she did.